CW01654592

GOOD Girl

M VIOLET

This book is a work of fiction. Names, characters, places, and incidents either are products of the author's imagination or used fictitiously. Any resemblance to actual events or locales, or persons, living or dead, is entirely coincidental and not intended by the author.

GOOD GIRL
M VIOLET

All Rights reserved. Except as permitted under the U.S. Copyright Act of 1976, no part of this publication may be reproduced, distributed, or transmitted in any form or by any means, or stored in a database or retrieval system, without prior consent and permission of the publisher.

Copyright © 2022 by M Violet

Cover Design by Sarah Paige. All stock photos licensed appropriately.

Edited by Kat's Literary Services

Formatted by Champagne Book Design

For information on subsidiary rights, please contact the publisher at authormviolet@gmail.com

Printed in the United States of America

A NOTE FROM THE AUTHOR

Good Girl is a dark romance meant for 18+ readers only. This is a short smutty novella very loosely inspired by Charles Dickens' A Christmas Carol. But this is not a retelling. And it's not about Christmas. This is something else. Extreme discretion advised. Please see the TWs below.

Trigger Warnings

*Graphic sexual scenes
*Graphic language
*Physical assault
*Sexual assault
*Coercion
*Dubious consent
*Sex with multiple partners
*Group sex
*Sword crossing
*Bondage
*Submission
*Kinks: choking, spanking, restraints, collar/leash, food play, praise, and degradation.

Playlist

"Haunted House"– Neoni

"Just Another Nightmare" – Fae

"Victim" – Halflives

"Motionless but Not Alone (Reaper)" – Andrea Viktoria

"You Made a Monster"– Nick Kingsley and Hannah Hart

"Run Baby Run" – The Rigs

"Faraway Far" – Mavenne

"The Foundations of Decay" – My Chemical Romance

"Smells Like Teen Spirit" – Malia J

"All the Dark Places" – Kat Leon and Jo Blankenburg

To spicy booktok. This one's for you.

GOOD *Girl*

Prologue

All Hallows' Eve

"You're not afraid of the dark, are you, Bailey?" My very sloppy drunk friend Maureen asked.

I laughed and threw back another lime green jello shot, tilting my head back so it could jiggle down my throat. "Hell no I'm not. That's where all the fun stuff happens."

Maureen hopped up on the center island next to me, her tits nearly falling out of her halter top in the process. "So you'll go then? Into the old Wickford place, by yourself with no flashlight?"

I rolled my eyes. "Are you still mad that I didn't want to dress up as a slutty witch with you? Is that why you are trying to ruin my Halloween Eve?"

Maureen laughed. "Oh, come on, Bailey. You know you want to. Besides, if the rumors are true, then you'll be getting fucked sideways just like you've always wanted. And your burlesque costume is just as slutty by the way."

I glanced down at my bustier right as Maureen made a grab for one of my breasts. I squealed and swatted her hand away playfully. "No more jello shots for you, missy," I teased.

"Seriously, though, Bailey. The party isn't until midnight, and I'm bored as fuck."

"Remind me again why Billy decided to throw a party so fucking late?"

"*Because* it's officially Halloween at midnight," Maureen whined as if that was the most ridiculous question I'd ever asked. "Now, let's go check out that creepy mansion and see what all the fuss is about."

I did love a good dare.

The old Wickford mansion had been the subject of superstition our whole lives. Last summer, after graduation, a bunch of kids got busted for throwing a party there and almost burning it down. The cops have since taped it off and it's scheduled to be demolished later this year.

Legend has it that every year on Halloween Eve, when the veil between the dead and the living fell down, three angry spirits demanded to be set free. They were locked away in one of the rooms there. Whoever let them out would be stuck with them until they gave them what they wanted. It was probably started by a bunch of horny frat boys who were just trying to lure unsuspecting drunk girls into the dark.

It sounded like a bunch of bullshit to me.

"Fine. Why not? It's not like any of that stuff is real. But you have to promise that you won't tell anyone about this later." Partying there with other people was one thing, roaming around by yourself like a weirdo was grounds to get labeled as such.

Maureen dipped one of her long pointy fingernails into another jello shot, scooping it out and sucking it off. "Shit, like *I'm* going to tell anyone. It will be our little secret, slut."

I shoved her a little too hard, and she toppled over. I reached out to catch her, and we both went tumbling to the floor, laughing. "Oh, fuck. Are we that drunk already?" I spurt out between hysterical bouts of laughter.

She pulled me on top of her and pretended to dry hump me. "Fuck yeah, bitch. You gonna set some spirits free tonight."

I pulled her up and steadied myself against the counter. "Alright, fuck. Let's go before I change my mind. Grab the rest of those shots for the walk over. I'm not doing this sober."

"Yay!" Maureen stumbled in front of me, trying not to drop the tray of shots as we left her house.

I fluffed my blonde hair as we walked, annoyed that the mist was starting to deflate my curls. I wanted to look hot tonight. To find some beautiful man at the party to make out with. Lord knows it had been way too long. But now I was traipsing through the streets in stiletto heels and fishnets, freezing my ass off. Hopefully we could go back to Maureen's house after and freshen up before the party.

The old Wickford house was a crumbling heap of decay. Just a hollow frame with barely anything left holding it together. I glanced up at the roof just in time to dodge a squirt of bird shit. It splattered on the cobblestones inches away from me.

Maureen howled with laughter. "Fuck, that almost landed on you."

There must have been a half a dozen birds' nests up there. "So gross," I groaned.

The rickety shutters banged against the house, creaking in the unforgiving wind. A shudder trickled up my spine. This place was creepy as fuck. "So what do I get for doing this stupid dare of yours?"

Maureen tapped a finger on her chin. "Hmm.. Let me think. Okay, if you go in there by yourself and manage to get that door unlocked, I'll let you call dibs on anyone you want at Billy's party tonight."

I rolled my eyes. "As if I need your permission on who I choose to make out with later."

She hissed. "Well, good luck trying with me pussy-blocking you all night."

Fuck. She would do it too. "Seriously, Maureen?"

She shrugged. "Fine. I'll let you borrow my red Balenciaga bag for a week."

A smirk pulled at my lips. That bag cost more than most people's rent. Her parents gave it to her for graduation. "All right. Deal. I go in alone and get the door open. Then I get dibs at the party *and* the Balenciaga bag."

"Both?" Maureen pouted.

I nodded. "And if I'm not out in fifteen minutes, you better come and get me, bitch. Psychos could be squatting in there."

A gust of wind rushed past us, blowing one of the shutters hard against the house. We both lurched back. Goosebumps prickled my arms. We should have brought coats, but no, we just had to be more concerned about how hot we looked.

An eerie sensation pulled at me. "I'm going to get you back good for this one, Maur," I called back to her as I moved toward the decaying porch. The wind picked up again, drowning out her response. All I could hear was the faint sound of giggling.

The floorboards creaked under my pointy high-heels. I was half-expecting to drive a hole straight through one of them. "I swear to god if I get my shoe caught in one of these things…" I cursed under my breath.

The house was empty, devoid of any furnishings or decorations. A little burst of adrenaline tingled through my veins. Ever since I was a kid, I'd been obsessed with horror movies and the occult. Walking around this spooky old house was so fucking dangerous, it almost turned me on.

I tested the railing as I started up the staircase, jiggling it to make sure it would hold. Using caution, I crept up the stairs, my heart pounding the closer I got to the top. Thanks to the busted-out windows, it was freezing inside. The wind howled through the house without anything to hinder it. It roamed wild and free. As if it lived here.

There were all sorts of sounds that would make a sane

person jump. Make them run out as fast as they could. Aside from the shutters banging against the house, there was the unsettling sound of rodents scratching the wood as they scurried up and down the walls. They never bothered me much, but Maureen, on the other hand, would have shrieked and leaped onto my back.

She never had the stomach for creepy things. Not like me. While I pretended to be annoyed or bored with her dares, I secretly relished them. The thrill of getting caught doing something dangerous was worth every second. I dreamed of things that would make grown men keel over. Dark and depraved things. Regular stuff bored me. I could only fuck missionary so many times before I'd die of boredom. Only so many of the same monotonous blow jobs I could give without wanting to scratch my own eyes out. I didn't want a normal guy. I wanted a monster. A deviant. Someone who could make me feel fucking alive for once.

But my type only existed in books and in my dreams. Hence why I was traipsing through a creepy condemned house without even a can of mace. For the thrill. The rush. It was the closest I could get to whatever it was I was looking for. That thing that I just couldn't grasp or name. *Fuck, I wish I could bottle this feeling.*

I paused at the top of the stairs and looked back over my shoulder. These abandoned houses tended to harbor less than savory characters. Despite my adrenaline addiction, having a run in with a crack-head or a serial killer was not what I had in mind.

Confident that no one was stalking me, I continued down the hall. The first two rooms I passed were empty just like the rest of the house. The doors torn off their hinges. Empty paper cups rolled around the floor, most likely remnants from that party a few weeks back. The doorframes were charred yet still looked sturdy enough to withstand a hurricane. That was the thing about these old houses—good bones.

The hall dead-ended with one last room. The only room that had a door still attached to it. I stood in front of it, and a chill snaked down my back. It was as if the temperature dropped another ten degrees in this spot. I've heard some people say that ghosts can make a room colder. The adrenaline junkie in me got off on that, but my inner skeptic was convinced it was just a wind tunnel, pulling the chill farther down.

I gasped as I wrapped my hand around the doorknob. It was ice cold. I tried to turn it, but it wouldn't budge.

"Come on," I groaned.

I jiggled it some more and leaned against the door but still nothing. I pulled out one of my hair pins and stuck it in the keyhole like they do in the movies, but I had no fucking clue what I was doing. *How the fuck is there still a locked door in an abandoned house?*

This is why that stupid superstition got started to begin with.

Fuck it.

I backed up a few steps and charged forward, slamming my body into the door. "Fuck," I cried out as I bounced off it. That was going to leave a fucking bruise. I really needed to stop thinking I was some kind of cat burglar.

I rubbed my shoulder, already feeling a lump forming.

This was pissing me off. It wasn't about the Balenciaga bag or first dibs on some vapid frat guy. No. I wanted that rush. *Needed it.* And I was just a tad bit curious to know if the legend was true. What if there really was three spirits in that room, ready to pounce on whoever let them out?

Waiting to do dark and dirty things. A tingling began between my thighs. *Only someone as fucked up as me would get aroused by that.*

I grabbed the doorknob again and jiggled it with all my might. "What the fuck?" I hissed. "Fucking open already." I slammed my hands on the door and sighed in defeat.

As I pulled out my phone to text Maureen that it wasn't happening, I started to turn when I felt a warm breath blow against the back of my neck. I whipped around, my heart racing, only to find no one there.

Fuck.

It felt like a man's breath. Footsteps thudded behind me. I spun around again just as a force rammed into me, knocking me backward. I crashed into the door like a wrecking ball. The wood splintered and gave way as I barreled through it.

"Oh, shit," I yelled.

I tumbled face forward and smacked my palms against the floorboards as I broke my own fall.

Okay, this was a bit more than adrenaline. Someone was fucking with me. I scrambled to my feet and glanced around only to find myself completely alone. There was no fucking way.

"Maureen?" I called out. "You better not be fucking with me, bitch."

My heart thudded in my chest. I ran to the open window and looked down. Maureen sat on a tree stump filing her nails. There was no way she could have run up here, pushed me, and then run back down in that amount of time.

I whirled around, the hairs on my neck standing straight up. It was dark. The wind had calmed to a whispering murmur, but the air was still freezing. Crisp and chill like a meat locker.

I snapped a quick picture of the broken door and darted back down the hall. The floor creaked behind me as if someone was following. I didn't bother to turn around this time. I flew down the steps, taking them two at a time. I ran as fast as one could in four-inch-high heels. But it was my adrenaline that carried me.

While I raced through the doorless entryway and down the front porch, I could barely catch my breath, my teeth chattering. Maureen leaped up from her stump to meet me, but I walked past her.

"Hey," she called out. "Did you do it?"

I didn't stop until we were a block away from the house, Maureen whining over the wind the whole time.

"Bailey, what the fuck happened?"

My hands trembled as I held up my phone. "It's done. I got in."

She nodded, arching an eyebrow at me. "Why do you look like you just saw a ghost?"

I didn't know what I saw or felt. But I wasn't alone up there. That was for fucking sure. "I don't want to talk about it. I just want to get really fucking drunk."

Maureen grinned and handed me a jello shot from the tray that I'd completely forgotten we'd brought. "Bottoms up."

I slammed three shots in a row on the walk back to Maureen's house. It wasn't enough to shake the eerie feeling of being watched. "Can we just stay here at your house tonight? I'm not in the mood to party with those assholes anymore."

Maureen stuck out her lower lip in a fake pout. "Don't be a downer, Bales. There will be plenty of drugs, alcohol, and chiseled abs to get you in the mood."

I shook my head. "Nah. I'm good. I think I'm coming down with something actually. I don't feel like being around a bunch of people."

She sighed and tipped back another jello shot. "Well, *I'm* going. I've been looking forward to this party all year."

I knew that if I told her what really happened she would stay. If I told her how freaked out I was, she wouldn't go. But I did have a bunch of shots before I stepped into that house, and my mind was probably just playing tricks on me. I didn't want to ruin her night just because I was coming down off a rush.

I nodded. "Okay, have fun, be safe, and use condoms. Call me tomorrow and tell me all the sordid details?"

Maureen planted a kiss on my cheek. "You know I will. Text me if you change your mind, bitch."

Lingering at her front gate, I watched her strut down the block toward Billy's house. A part of me was tempted to follow. But I just couldn't shake this feeling that had crept into my skin. I wanted a hot shower, a stiff drink, and to forget this night ever happened.

CHAPTER One

It was midnight.

Happy fucking Halloween to me.

I wiped away the steam from the mirror and knocked back another shot of whiskey. I had brought the bottle with me. But despite the hot shower and copious amounts of booze, I could not escape this chill in my bones. It gripped me.

I slipped on a pair of black lace panties and my favorite T-shirt. It was big enough to cover my ass but not enough to keep me very warm. But all my sweatpants were still in the washer. I'd been so excited to go out with Maureen tonight that I had forgotten to change them over to the dryer.

Fuck me.

I scurried into my bed and pulled the thick blankets up around my chin. It wouldn't be long before I'd be hot and throwing them off anyway. I was disappointed that I didn't have a hard cock against my ass right now, though. Ugh, I should have gone to the party.

It was just a few minutes after midnight. Maybe I could still muster up the energy to go? I know I'd have a good time. And maybe it was what I needed to shake off this creepy sensation that had followed me all the way home from that fucking cursed mansion.

As I lay there contemplating getting dressed again and going out, movement flashed in my periphery. What the fuck?

My breath hitched as I laid as still as possible. Was I imagining things in the dark now? A soft wind brushed past me. And then I saw it.

The shadow moved across my bedroom.

It growled, breathing heavy. It stretched as it got closer. My stomach flipped. This was no shadow, but a man with broad shoulders.

I gasped as he came closer and towered over my bed. I shivered, terrified yet aroused.

What was wrong with me?

His green eyes peered down at me, filled with lust and malice. Like he fucking hated me. Like he wanted to own me.

I was afraid to breathe. Afraid to move.

He leaned over me and pressed his fists into the mattress, boxing me in. His lips hovered over mine. "Do you understand what's about to happen? I'm going to do bad things to you, Bailey. Dirty, filthy, depraved things. And you're going to like it. And you're not going to beg me to stop. You'll demand me to finish. You know why? Because the brutality makes you feel alive. You've been dying in your own skin for so long. That ends tonight. I've come to awaken every vile piece of you."

Oh, fuck.

He wrapped his strong hands around my wrists and yanked me from my bed, tossing me onto the floor. I gasped as he kept coming, stalking toward me. I scrambled back, my heart pounding.

But where would I go? I couldn't run. No. Not from him. He would never let me get far.

He hissed, his lips pursed, as he dug his fingers into my hair. "This way, little fox."

I yelped as he dragged me across the floor by my strands. "You don't get to cum in your own bed. Not yet. You cum when and where I say you can. When *we* say you can."

We? Oh, fuck. *There is more of them?*

My skin burned against the carpet as he pulled me across it. He kicked open doors as he dragged me. We passed through rooms that used to belong to me. This was his house now. There was no escape. I had done this to myself.

We stopped in the living room. Two other shadows lurked in the dark. Their breaths were heavy. I could sense their arousal. Their lust. *Fuck, fuck, fuck.* Did I want this? Did I have a choice?

The man's fingers twisted in my hair, pulling me up to a half crouch. "This is your life for now, little fox. You live at our mercy. Time to see how well you behave."

A second man growled. "Take off her clothes. Show us what we've won."

I hugged my arms to my chest as the man with the black hair and green eyes hovered over me. A sinister chuckle erupted from deep in his gut. He trailed a finger across my jaw, so soft as if he were the gentlest man in existence. He was not.

"Do you deny us our release, little fox?"

I trembled as he crouched down, putting himself at eye level with my clenched pussy. The only thing covering it was my thin lace panties. Why was this making me so wet?

"We can't force you, but we aren't leaving until we get what we want. The sooner you give in to your own desires, the sooner you admit your carnal appetite to yourself, then the fun can begin. And when we've had our fill, we'll leave you alone forever."

I can't believe that fucking curse is real. What a stupid fucking girl I was. But in my defense, who would actually believe that unlocking a door in a supposedly haunted house would send three scary—though hot as hell—spirits to my house in the middle of Halloween night? Three angry spirits with tattoos and chiseled abs who have been sex starved for centuries.

But he just revealed a secret. They can't make me do anything. Sure, they can torment me and occupy my house for the rest of my life, but they can't *make* me do anything. But would they really have to?

As I looked each one up and down, my nipples pebbling at the sight of their wild eyes already undressing me, their heaving chests practically panting for me, I wondered, would they really have to make me do anything? What if he was right?

Maybe I wanted this just as much as they did. Maybe more. They weren't the only ones who had been starving for sexual touch. I craved it. And I would be lying to myself if I didn't admit that my fantasies lately have started just like this. Only this time, it was real.

CHAPTER Two

My heart pounded. "I'm not taking my clothes off for you." I wasn't ready. "I don't even know your names."

The dark haired one smiled, looking back and winking at the other two who sat perched on my living room windowsill. "She makes an excellent point."

He sat down next to me, and I flinched as he wrapped an arm around my shoulders. His grip was hard and firm, the muscles flexing to show me just how strong he was. "You can call me Poe." He pointed to the blond, blue eyed one, the one with the deep scar going through his eyebrow. "That's Grim."

Poe nodded toward the third disturbingly sexy man-spirit who had yet to utter a single word. He just glared at me hungrily with his sharp brown eyes. He barely moved a muscle except for when he was running his tattooed hand through his dirty blond locks. "And that silent beauty over there, he's called Saint... I assure you he's anything but."

Grim growled as he fingered the buckle of his belt. "Now she can choose which name to scream out when we're defiling that tight little cunt of hers."

Saint licked his lips, his throat bobbing as he swallowed. But he remained quiet. And this is why he scared me the most. The silent assassin, watching me like I was a bird in a cage. A cage that only they held the key to.

What the fuck did I let out last night?

My breath hitched. "So you want me to have sex with all three of you? Are you insane? You break into my house and tell me I have to fuck you. This is absurd. I will *scream*."

Poe grabbed my throat and whispered in my ear, "Yes. You will."

Grim chuckled. "But no one will hear you, little fox. Not out here."

Poe tightened his hold on me. "Starting to regret moving out to the woods?" he drawled.

I should run. Call for help. But where? There's no way I'd outrun them. Even if I could, no one would care. They'd say I deserved it. It was no secret that I'd had my share of men in this town. It was okay for them, but I was the one who was judged for it. *Bastards*.

Poe pulled me into his chest. His other hand rested on my bare thigh. Heat radiated off of him. His breath tickled my ear as he whispered, "It will be so much more than sex, little fox." He nodded at Grim, who stalked over and sat on the other side of me.

Grim nestled in close. His hard body was like a brick wall against mine. He placed his hand on my other thigh, higher up than Poe's, and squeezed. "This is the fucking nightmare you've dreamed about," Grim rasped in my ear.

His fingers inched further up, lingering at the edge of my panties. "A part of you wanted it to be true. That's why you opened the door. I can fucking smell your sweet, little, wet cunt from here. I can feel the pulse in your leg, hammering, aching for us to give you what you've never had."

"No," I rasped, shaking my head. No, no, no. This couldn't be real. There was no such thing as ghosts. These were just three run of the mill, albeit sexy as fuck, psychos.

Grim slid his free hand to the nape of my neck, tangling his fingers in my damp strands. He jerked my head back and hovered over my mouth, licking his lips as he watched me tremble. "You *will* let us play with you. *You'll beg us to.*"

I was completely pinned yet neither would make a move until I gave permission. It was terrifying and arousing at the same time. I clenched my pussy tight. *Damn my body for betraying me like this.*

Saint finally stirred. He slowly rose from my windowsill and ambled forward. His lips curled up into a smirk that was so heavily laced with lust and malice that I almost had a fucking heart attack. Saint planted himself across from me, using my coffee table as a chair. He pushed my legs apart and scooted closer, forcing himself into my space.

Grim shoved my head toward Saint until our lips were almost touching. Adrenaline spiked through me as his breath danced across my face. Saint let out a low growl, so soft I almost thought my ears were playing tricks on me.

His fingers dug into the sides of my knees as he kept me from retreating. "*Say yes*," he breathed.

Poe nodded. "We have all the time in the world, little fox. If you won't let us begin, there are other ways we can torture you..."

Fuck.

As soon as he said it, I knew that they would make good on that promise. They were so beautiful it hurt to look them in the eyes. Brutal fucking savages with unsatiable appetites. But it made me feel something dark and twisted and fucking alive. I could take from them as much as I wanted. *What I've always wanted.* But what would they do to me? How deep down the dark rabbit hole was I willing to go?

But I couldn't make that mistake again. To trust. Not like that night in the back of my ex-boyfriend's truck. The one time I tried to explore my desires, tried to show him what I wanted, and he called me a slut.

When he accused me of fucking everyone he knew. Because how could a chaste girl like me possibly know what I wanted sexually? Surely if I knew how to touch myself, how to ask for what I wanted, then I must be a slut, right? *Fucking simple-minded asshole.* He had been my first of many after that night. A string of boring one-night stands where my excitement was as fleeting as my orgasms.

I squirmed out of their grip, twisting out of Grim's hold on my hair and swatting Poe and Saint's hands away. "You don't know anything about what I want," I snapped.

They let me stand.

I moved away from them, toward the window seat, shivering with nothing to keep me warm without their body heat except a thin white T-shirt that barely covered my ass.

Poe smiled at Grim. With a quick nod, he was on his feet, crossing the distance between us. I shrunk back against the throw pillows.

Grim stopped just inches in front of me. "Let the torture begin."

CHAPTER Three

I held my breath as he unbuckled his belt and slowly slid it out of its loops. I jumped as he snapped it in front of him. "Let's see how much wetter I can get you, little fox."

My heart hammered in my throat. What the fuck was he going to do?

Grim unbuttoned his jeans, pushed them down, and stepped out of the rumpled fabric, kicking them across the room. I gasped at the sight of his smooth, hard cock standing at attention.

He chuckled as he peeled off his black T-shirt, revealing his beautifully carved body. There wasn't a single flaw. With a six pack of abs and two steel rods piercing through his nipples, he looked like a runway model. Only his dark sinister gaze reminded me what he really was.

A predator.

Grim stood completely naked in front of me while Poe and Saint looked on, leaning back and seemingly enjoying the show. Grim moved closer, forcing my legs apart with his knees as he towered over me.

Fuck. He was gorgeous.

I gasped as he wrapped his left hand around my throat, firm but not hard enough to restrict my breath. The feel of his grip on my neck had me clenching again. *Why did this turn me on so much?*

My heart skittered as I anticipated his next move. Was he going to force me to suck his cock? Would I even put up much of a fight? I was practically salivating over it.

His eyes hardened and his lips pulled tight. "Watch," he commanded.

"Watch what?" I murmured.

He fisted his cock with his right hand and began stroking his shaft up and down. I tilted my chin up to look away from his throbbing cock, and he gave my throat a quick squeeze. "*I said, fucking watch.*"

"Oh, shit," I whimpered, struggling for breath. I nodded and he relaxed his grip on me slightly.

"*Good girl.*"

He began stroking his cock again, back, and forth. He circled the tip with his thumb, pinching it between his fingers as a little spurt of pre-cum pooled out.

"You want a taste, don't you, little fox? You want to slide those pouty lips up and down my cock until they're bruised and swollen. If you say otherwise, than you're a fucking liar," he breathed.

Was he right?

I couldn't move or look away. Heat flooded my body as he took his time, languishing in each stroke of his veiny shaft. My nipples ached as they pebbled against the cotton of my shirt, imagining what his hands could do to them. My panties were soaked.

"Say yes, little fox. Just one word and I'll give you what you want. I can see your swollen nipples through that sweat-soaked shirt. I know they're aching to be sucked."

Grim squeezed my throat a little tighter. "*Aching* to feel the scrape of my teeth against them."

Oh, fuck.

Sweat beaded down my back. I was falling apart. Unraveling. Every breath shorter than the last. I kept my eyes glued to his glistening cock, for fear that if I looked into his eyes he'd know. That everything he said was true. That I wanted him. I wanted all three of them.

I fisted my hands at my sides as his breaths grew more rapid. He let out a soft moan and rubbed himself harder, faster. Tingles erupted inside my aching pussy. Watching him, as he held me in place with one hand and fondled himself with the other was vicious. It was fucking brutal. But only because I would not let myself give in.

"Uhh," he moaned. "Fuck. Get ready for it, little fox."

What the… oh, fuck. He grunted and moved his hand to the back of my neck. I whimpered as he tugged my head back and released his cum on my throat. It came out thick and hot. Dripped down my shirt. I quivered as it oozed in between my breasts. I stared at the ceiling as he surrendered to his orgasm, feeling his warm sticky cum drip all over me.

He yanked my head hard and rubbed his fingers over my neck, smearing his cum across my jaw and over my tightly closed lips. I would not give in, dammit. *But fuck how I wanted to.*

Grim pulled me upright, smiled and stepped back. "I look good on you, little fox."

Poe rose and stalked over to us. My heartbeat fast. He took a seat next to me. "We can keep playing these games, or you can give us what we want. *What you want.*"

I looked around the room, soaking in their hungry stares. They didn't look like ghosts. No. They were solid and formed like men. Beautiful men. Poe with his black hair and green eyes, the way they slinked over every inch of me like I was about to be devoured.

Then Grim, the tallest of the three. His black and grey tattoos swirled and climbed over almost every inch of his skin, highlighting every inch of his hard muscled body. The sexy V-shape that dipped down below his abs, aching to be licked. His blonde hair was slicked back off his forehead revealing the undersides shaved and imprinted with more tattoos. His blue eyes pierced me like razors.

And finally, Saint, he was the biggest of the three. Not in height but in stature. He looked like a bouncer or like he belonged in some fight club. His dirty blond hair was tied up in a top knot. Shadows flickered behind his brown eyes.

A tremor shot through me as Poe stroked my cheek with the tip of his finger. "Give in to your desire, little fox. Let us give you what you've been too scared to get for yourself."

My heart hammered. I could barely control my breath. "I-I'm not scared."

Grim stepped back into his black jeans, pulling them up slowly. He tucked his cock back inside but left the zipper and button undone. He stood over me and cupped my chin in his hand. "You're terrified, Bailey. And it makes you so fucking wet, you couldn't clench your legs together any tighter if you tried."

I tried to swallow, but my throat was so dry. "I need a drink."

Saint made his way into the kitchen and returned with a bottle of wine and a glass. He poured it and as he handed it to me, he kept his fingers curled around the stem. I inhaled a sharp breath as his skin grazed mine. "This will help you relax, little fox."

Or it would just make me make stupider decisions.

I gulped down half of it in one sip. "This is great. Just fucking great. I'm being haunted by three sex starved ghosts. How is that even possible? This can't be real."

Poe inched himself closer to me. "Stop talking. There are better uses for that sexy mouth of yours."

Grim nodded, heat rising in his stare. "Open up for us. We've waited a long time for you, Bailey. Our sly little fox..."

Why were they calling me that? "No. Please, just leave. I can't give you what you want."

Poe sighed. "Wrong answer."

I gasped as he yanked me to my feet. He whipped me around and pulled me to him. His stiff cock ground against my back. Without warning he walked me forward into the wall and pressed harder into me. He fisted my hair tight in his palm. He pressed my face to the wall and breathed heavy into my ear. "You're the only one who can give us what we want."

He smelled so fucking good. I whimpered as he reached around and began slowly pulling up the edges of my shirt. "Spread your legs, little fox."

I wriggled against him, trying to squirm out of his hold but all that did was make him grip me tighter. He shoved his foot between my ankles and knocked them apart, forcing me to widen my stance. My clit ached as he pressed me further into the wall. "Tell me you're not wet right now, and I'll let you go."

I grunted in frustration. "I'm not wet."

He ran his teeth over my earlobe as he whispered, "Liar."

"Prove it, little fox," Grim taunted. "Let him touch you."

Oh, fuck. I wanted to be touched so bad.

I squirmed again. Poe pressed into me. I could feel the hem of my shirt getting higher. My panties were exposed now. My legs spread open. He stroked my belly in soft small circles with his fingers. I quivered. "*Fuck,*" I whispered underneath my breath.

"Relax, little fox. Let me touch you," Poe rasped.

I was practically panting. I'd never been exposed like this. This vulnerable. I bit down on my lower lip and shook my head. "I-I don't want you to."

He snickered and released me. "Liar," he repeated.

I turned around and leaned back against the wall. "You don't know me."

Poe twirled a lock of my blonde hair. "We know you better than you know yourself. The sooner you give into what you want, the more alive we'll all be."

He stalked away and sat down on the couch while keeping his feral gaze on me.

Saint smirked. I didn't even realize he was capable of any expression. "Aren't you tired of always being in control, Bailey? Hmm?" He grabbed a black duffel bag from behind the couch that I hadn't noticed until now.

He unzipped it slowly. "We can do things to you that even your wildest fantasies couldn't muster."

I clenched my pussy again, praying my slick juices didn't pool any farther down my thighs. "What do you want to do to me?" I asked, terrified and more aroused than I'd ever been in my whole life.

Saint reached inside the bag and pulled out a black leather riding crop. He caressed the tip of it and then smacked it against his palm. I flinched.

"You think you're wet now, little fox… Submit to us. Say yes, and you will feel pleasure unlike any you've ever known," Saint breathed.

My legs began to shake. I had never been spanked before. But I'd be lying to myself if I said I hadn't always wanted to be. Fuck. How did they seem to know all the dirty things I wanted done to me?

CHAPTER *Four*

I'd heard about fight or flight moments, but this wasn't that. In this moment, it was either fuck or flight. And what was really starting to scare me was how I didn't want to flee at all. But I should. I needed to. What kind of girl would I be if I let three strangers do dark and dirty things to me? It was shameful. I needed to take care of this myself before I exploded.

"I-I need a second." I shot past them and darted for the bathroom. I was almost to the door when Saint caught my wrist.

"Shit."

He pushed me back against the wall and pinned my wrists above my head. He sniffed my hair like a wolf about to attack its prey. "Don't close that door."

"Excuse me? I have to pee. I'm not doing that with the door open." I could feel my cheeks heating.

Saint twisted his fingers around my wrists. "Liar. You and I both know what you are going in there to do. But if you want to make yourself cum, you'll have to do it in front of us."

Fuck. Of course, they knew. No matter how much my mouth protested, my body gave them every ounce of proof they needed to know I was aching for release.

"Or do one better, and let *us* make you cum," Poe chimed in as he approached, admiring Saint's grip on me.

Grim joined us now too. I was surrounded, pinned against my own hallway wall. By all three of them. Trapped, with Grim's cum still all over me. And I was disgustingly, ridiculously, viciously aroused.

"Please, just let me go," I murmured. *Please don't.*

Grim stroked my cheek. "You belong to us, little fox. Time to accept it."

Poe nodded. "There's no shame in wanting this. Let us show you."

"Say yes." Saint pleaded.

My head spun. My heart hammered. Every inch of my body was on fire with lust. Every nerve ending erect and aware of their effect on me. I was wetter than rain, my nipples ached, my clit throbbed in anticipation. This is what I'd fantasized about. It was finally happening.

So why was I so afraid to give in?

Grim lifted my shirt, exposing my belly while Poe traced the edges of my panties, taunting me. "Let us inside, little fox. I want to feel that tight little cunt clench around my fingers."

Grim placed his hand on the small of my back, tracing small circles over the base of my spine. "Spread your legs, little fox. Open up," he rasped.

Saint lowered his lips to mine, stopping just short of kissing me. "Submit… *Say. Yes.*"

A blast of sensations hit me at once. Heat spread between my legs. Sweat dripped from every crevice. I panted at the stimulation of all three of them surrounding me, teasing me, begging me to give in.

"Fuck…I-I just…" The scent of their sweat mixed with night and musk and desire was overwhelming. It was seductive and every inch of my skin was raw. Tingling. Every nerve twitched at the thought of giving up control to them.

Poe pulled at the edges of my panties a little firmer but still holding back. "You're so close to the edge, little fox… time to jump."

My chest heaved. I couldn't take it anymore. I took deep breaths, locking eyes with each of them as I did. The tension in the room grew thick as they waited. As they watched my chest rise and fall. As they watched my lips tremble.

I swallowed and willed moisture back into my mouth, but all I could muster was a throaty whisper, "*Yes…*"

A collective swoosh of air peeled back as all three of them pressed in closer to me. Poe slipped a finger inside my panties, stilling it right above my swollen clit. "*Good girl.*"

Grim cupped my ass and gave it a hard pinch. "You

belong to us now, little fox. Every single piece of your flesh belongs to us."

Saint wrapped his hand around my throat, and I flinched slightly. Was I really ready for this?

He held firm. "You're no longer in control, Bailey. We're going to do whatever we want with you."

I couldn't catch my breath. "What-what are you going to do?"

"Shh… Let's get you more comfortable," Poe hushed in my ear.

Saint reached into his back pocket and pulled out a switchblade. He grabbed the hem of my shirt and cut into it, dragging the blade up in short little jerks as it tore through the fabric. I leaned back against the wall as Grim and Poe each held one of my wrists over my head.

Saint split my shirt wide open, the air hit my nipples and I gasped.

"So fucking beautiful…" He traced the tip of the blade delicately across my collarbone.

He tipped my chin up with the blade. "Say it."

I looked back and forth between the three of them, confused.

Grim growled in my ear. "Say you belong to us."

This was it. I had made my decision. I couldn't escape it. And I didn't want to. I licked my lips. "I'm yours. God help me, but I belong to you now."

Saint nodded at Poe. He flashed me a grin as he dipped a finger below my panty line, sliding it down my slick slit. I moaned as he pressed against my nub. "So fucking wet for us. I knew you were a fucking liar. But now you're going to be a good girl, aren't you?"

I bit down on my lip as he slid his finger in and out my pussy, slowly. It was agonizing. I nodded. "Yes, I'll be a good girl."

Poe drew in a sharp breath. "Go sit on the couch."

I staggered over to my brown leather cushions and started to sit down when Grim called for me to stop. "Panties off. I want to see that sweet cunt bare against the leather."

Saint was behind me in seconds. I felt the press of the blade against my thigh, then the pull from it ripping the fabric of my panties wide open and away from me.

"*That's better,*" Grim growled.

My legs were shaking. I was completely naked, vulnerable, and exposed for all three of them to see.

And they eyed me like prey, hungrily.

I sat on the couch, perched on the edge, my knees locked together.

Saint came from behind and grabbed my shoulders. "Relax, little fox. Lean all the way back."

Oh god, I really was giving up control now. I didn't resist as he pulled my shoulders into the cushions.

Grim and Poe retook their positions on either side of me.

"Open up, little fox. I want to see everything," Poe murmured.

I spread my legs apart just as Saint's hands slid down my chest and cupped my breasts. I gasped as he pinched both my nipples between his fingers, rubbing them back and forth. I could feel the heat flooding me, the intensity of his grip driving my body to near convulsions.

"That's our good girl. So naughty. You're our dirty girl, too, aren't you?" Grim asked.

I licked my lips, my throat dry. "Um... I-I don't know," I squeaked out.

Grim dragged his tongue across my jaw. "Yes, you do. You're so fucking filthy. So beautifully dirty. Say it."

My nipples swelled as Saint pinched and rolled them tight between his fingers. It was getting harder to concentrate on what stimulation was coming from where.

Grim jerked my chin and kissed me hard. "I asked you a question, little fox."

"Yes... I'm a dirty girl," I panted.

Grim snickered. "You know what happens to dirty girls, Bailey? *Hmm?*... Dirty. Fucking. Things."

Poe locked eyes with Grim, a sinister smirk flashed on both their faces. "Open her up for me."

CHAPTER *Five*

I had never been with more than one man at the same time.

He was right. It *was* dirty. But I didn't want it to stop.

I drew in a sharp breath as Grim pulled back the lips of my pussy. "Uhh," I whimpered.

Poe teased my entrance with his long fingers and without warning, shoved one inside.

"Fuck yeah, little fox. You're so wet for us. So ready."

I gasped as Saint pinched my nipples harder. Grim stroked the outside of my pussy, pressing his thumb on my swollen nub as Poe pushed his finger deeper inside me. I couldn't breathe.

Ripples of ecstasy hit me, wave after wave as I struggled to remain in control of my body. I was going to cum faster than I'd even thought possible. Grim stretched me wider apart as Poe inserted a second finger. I clenched my walls around him and screamed from the pleasure.

"It's too much," I panted.

"Shh, relax. You're doing so fucking good." He pumped his fingers in and out.

I arched my hips, rolling against his hand. "*Fuck,* that feels… amazing."

Grim rubbed the outside of my pussy, gliding his fingers through my slick folds. "This is just the beginning, little fox."

Without warning, Saint released my breasts. Grim spun me sideways so I was laying across the couch in his lap, my back against his chest. His cock stiffened and pulsed against my ass.

Poe hovered over me; the length of his torso wedged between my thighs. This was fucking insane and exhilarating. He kissed my belly, dragging the tip of his tongue down my wet slit. His tongue was soft and hot and firm.

Saint came around the side, a rope dangling in his hands. He grabbed my wrists. I panted as he held them over my head and fastened the rope tight around them. He tied the other end of the rope to a leg of the couch.

I couldn't move. And it fucking drove me wild. This was truly giving up control. I was at their mercy.

Grim drew light circles around my nipples with his fingertips. "Such a good fucking girl. About to burst so we can all taste that sweet cum of yours."

"Oh shit," I rasped.

Poe worked my pussy with his tongue, licking and

sucking and scraping his teeth gently across my folds. I bucked wildly, flailing as the overstimulation pushed me to the edge.

Saint kneeled down beside me. "Arch her up."

With his tongue buried deep inside me, Poe lifted my hips, making a space for Saint to wedge his hand between me and Grim. Grim squeezed my breasts while Saint yanked Grim's pants down and fisted his cock.

"*Fuck*, Saint, that's right," Grim moaned. Saint guided Grim's shaft up and down the line of my ass, sandwiching it between my needy flesh. Poe sucked my clit harder. I clenched around him, feeling every single pulse and flick.

I cried out as my orgasm began to climb inside me. Grim squeezed my nipples tight as he sucked on my earlobe. Saint pushed down on my abdomen with one hand while he rubbed my ass raw with Grim's huge stiff cock in his other hand.

"Little fox..." Saint breathed. He pressed down on my belly. "You have no idea how dirty I'm going to get you."

I moaned as the pressure built. They were right. I could never have dreamt this up. This was unfathomable. I was over stimulated.

With Grim's smooth shaft wedged between my ass, sliding up and down, seeking entrance. Poe's tongue devouring me like I was a bowl of his favorite ice cream. And Saint. The one who barely speaks, orchestrating it all. He was barely touching me, but I was most aroused by him.

"Oh fuck, I'm...com...coming." I screamed and arched my back, ignoring the burns around my wrists as I pulled on my restraints.

The three of them nestled in close, not letting up as all the blood in my body rushed to my head. Stars studded my vision as I moaned out the longest and most satisfying orgasm I'd ever had.

"Fuucckk…"

They stroked me as I came down.

"Breathe, little fox. Don't want to wear you out just yet," Poe cooed.

Grim adjusted himself underneath me, while Saint untied me and pushed me back up to a sitting position.

"We have so much more planned for you," Saint rasped.

I was so dizzy I almost blacked out. It was better than my fantasy. And I knew that the night was just beginning. This sent a tingling sensation back to my middle, as I still rode out the wave of my orgasm. I wanted more.

Poe cupped my face and pulled my face to his. "I want you to taste yourself on my tongue." He kissed me without warning, and I melted into him. Tasting myself was so naughty. So fucking dirty. I nearly came again.

Grim rubbed my back as Poe explored my mouth, his kisses deepening with every whimper I let out. When he finally broke away, he stole my breath with him. I felt like I was on fire.

"Tell us, little fox," Grim urged, "Why are you afraid of your own pleasure? Hmm?" His hands were tangled in my hair. He stroked the back of my neck. It was soothing and stimulating at the same time.

I was ashamed to answer. "Not everyone likes what I like."

Poe wrapped his hand around my throat and planted a kiss on my jaw. "*We* are what you fucking like, baby girl. And we are right fucking here to worship you. Don't be afraid."

Saint nodded. "You're beautiful."

There was a strange connection between me and Saint. At first I didn't even think he liked me. Now I was starting to wonder. He took such care with me. As if I would break in his hands. I'd let him fucking break me if he wanted to. I craved him most of all.

But something else was bothering me. Despite my lack of belief in ghosts and spirits, I know what I felt back at Wickford mansion. I *know* something unseen pushed me into that door. I hadn't had that many jello shots to where I would hallucinate that.

I curled my legs to my chest, blanketing myself with my own body. "What happened to the three of you? Why are you... dead?"

Grim's breath hitched. He moved my arms and replaced them with his. "Don't cover yourself. If you're cold, we'll keep you warm."

His strong arms wrapped around me, protectively. He hugged me to his chest, placing one arm across my breasts while cupping my pussy with the other. A new wave of tingles shot through me at the instant heat from his palm.

Grim chuckled. "Relax, little fox. They'll be plenty more of that later. This is just to keep the heat flowing in all the right places."

The warmth spread to my belly. My nipples pebbled underneath his forearm. Fuck. "You're trying to distract me," I breathed.

Poe smirked as he fixated on the way Grim was holding me. "And it's working, isn't it?"

Saint grunted as he stood up. "She needs nourishment. I'll get her something to eat and drink."

I couldn't help but squirm a bit against Grim's palm. It radiated like fire through my pussy. I wanted to grind against it. To feel my orgasm climb again. It felt so fucking good.

Grim tsked in my ear. "Such a dirty girl. Don't think I can't feel you trying to rub against me."

My breath grew heavy. "I'm just cold."

"Lie all you want, little fox, but your cunt tells the truth." Poe lounged back against the other end of the couch and pulled off his shirt.

I gasped. His chest was perfect. Carved like stone. "I'm not lying." I was.

Saint returned with a glass of water and a bowl of fruit. He sat down on the coffee table again and set the bowl beside him. "Drink." He handed me the water and I obeyed.

Grim slid his arm back and forth across my breasts. "Good girl."

Saint then picked out a peach and began carving it with his knife. I reached out to take a slice when Poe snatched it from him instead. He dangled the juicy fruit over my lips. "You are not in control anymore. Remember?"

I nodded, my heart racing.

He rubbed the fruit against my lips. "Open your mouth."

As soon as I parted my lips, he shoved the peach slice in. It tasted like heaven. Like fucking ecstasy. Not because it was a good piece of fruit but because Poe had fed it to me. I was practically purring.

Saint started to feed me another slice when Poe stopped him. "You know what, Saint? I feel like something is missing… Grim, what would make our good girl enjoy her meal more?"

His grip on my pussy tightened, reinvigorating the need between my thighs. "Her cunt is as wet as that peach. Would you like to see?"

Poe nodded. "Mmm, very much."

"Make her cum for us," Saint growled.

Oh fuck. My senses were back into overdrive.

Grim shifted his hand and slowly started to caress my outer folds. I parted my legs wider as he stroked, needing to feel every inch of him inside me.

"Grim, please," I panted.

Saint brought a slice of peach to my lips but didn't relinquish it. "Suck."

I moaned as the sweet peach filled my mouth. I sucked on Saint's fingers as he held it, the fruit between my lips.

"Fucking hell, little fox," Poe cried out. "I want a taste."

I gasped as Poe grabbed another slice of the bright tangy fruit and dragged it down my pussy, slathering the juices across my skin. I trembled as the sticky juice coated me and the soft flesh tickled my clit.

"Do you like that, little fox? How does it feel to be so fucking dirty?"

I arched back, panting. "Don't fucking stop," I pleaded.

Poe chuckled as he shoved the fruit that was now

coated in my cum into his mouth. He moaned as he savored it. "Fuck, you taste so good."

Grim slipped a finger inside my pussy. "I don't think you're dirty enough, little fox." He pumped another finger in, hooking up toward my G-spot.

I moaned. Oh, fuck. My head was buzzing. Still sucking on Saint's juice covered fingers, I spread my legs as far as they could go. Grim pulled the lips of my pussy back. He slid his fingers up and down my slit, then in and out, while Poe licked every trace of peach juice off me. I bucked my hips, arching up as he pressed down hard on my clit with his thumb.

Poe's eyes fixated on all of it. "Fuck, yeah. Just like that, Grim."

He moaned into my ear. "You're so fucking tight."

Poe gripped my thighs, digging his fingers into the side of my knees, and spreading me wider apart. "You want it harder, don't you, little fox? Faster?"

Saint grunted, fisting his own cock, rubbing himself as he watched us.

"Tell him, little fox," Poe repeated.

I was going to black out. The pressure was building to the point where I couldn't even see straight. "Fuck, yes. Harder. Please, Grim."

"Oh, fuck." Grim pushed his fingers deeper inside, pumping so fast I could barely breathe.

Poe stroked the inside of my thighs. "That's our good girl. So fucking good."

White lights sparked in my vision as my orgasm

rumbled from the center of me and burst out. I clenched around his fingers and screamed.

"Fuck," I whispered as I came down, trying to reclaim my breath. "Fuck..."

I rolled my head to the side to look at Saint. His dick was still hard as a rock, but he was no longer holding it as it tented his pants. He let out a deep quivering breath and closed his eyes for a moment. "I'm not ready to cum yet."

He handed me the glass of water and I drank it down in one sip. That was already two orgasms in the span of one hour. That had never happened to me before. No one had ever even bothered trying before.

My head was spinning. "I'm going to need more sustenance than just a couple of peach slices. And I'd like to at least wear my robe."

Poe started to protest, but I cut him off. "I think I've been a *very good girl*. I've earned a respite for a little bit."

Saint nodded. "Yes, she's right."

Grim smiled devilishly down at me. "Already making demands and owning what you want. I knew you were fucking perfect."

Poe got to his feet. "I'll be right back with a robe for our sly little fox."

As the night carried on, I was beginning to realize that as much as I belonged to them, *they belonged to me*. I was their good girl, but they were my beautiful savage devils. We would break each other. And then we'd put each other back together.

CHAPTER *Six*

I sat on the edge of the windowsill with a steaming cup of coffee, my fluffy gray robe tied tight around me. I gazed out the window, getting lost in that space between dusk and dawn. When the sky was a dark blue. It was the quietest time of day. Not even the birds were awake yet.

The guys watched me intently from across the room. Their breathing growing heavy again as they looked on. I felt the tingling begin to stir again. Knowing how bad they wanted me. Was I just as insatiable as them?

I locked eyes with Poe. "Tell me what happened to you. How did you die?"

"We were poisoned," Poe snarled.

"All three of you?" I asked. "When? Who poisoned you?"

"So many questions," Grim drawled. "Let's just enjoy our time together. The past doesn't matter."

"I want to know." I raised my chin in defiance.

"It was a long time ago, Bailey," Saint grumbled.

Poe licked his lips. "Keep being a good girl and maybe I'll tell you what happened." The way his gaze traveled over the length of my body was enough to make me shiver.

"I need to use the bathroom."

Poe nodded. "Don't linger in there too long though, or I'll have to drag you out."

I shuddered and reminded myself that they were predators. No matter how gorgeous or sexy, or how skilled they were with their tongues, they were apex predators. And I had bargained with them. Traded my body for their souls. The night was far from over.

I shut the door behind me and thought better about locking it. That wouldn't keep them out anyway. It would only piss them off. I couldn't lie that the hint of danger, and their impulsive tempers sent a little shiver up my spine. A *tingling* shiver that stirred up a fresh sheen of moisture between my legs. What was wrong with me? Had I been alone so long that any attention was turning me on. Even from vile delicious spirits who refuse to leave until I let them defile my body?

I was as fucked in the head as they were.

After splashing some water on my face, I rested my trembling hand on the doorknob. I wanted more but I was still a bit terrified. What if I couldn't handle any more?

As I turned the knob and opened the door, I gasped, almost walking right into Grim. He stood, blocking the doorway, naked and waiting for me.

He held a leather collar in his hands. "Come here, little fox."

I shook my head. "What is that?"

"A gift," he drawled.

I backed up into the bathroom, ashamed and horrified that the sight of it in his hands made me wet again.

Grim stalked forward, his eyes ablaze with renewed hunger. "I like hunting you, little fox. These games you play are so fucking hot. Pretending you don't want the same things. You make me so hard."

He backed me up until there was nowhere to go. The cold wall hit my back, and I froze. "What is that for?"

Grim smirked and held the collar up closer so I could see its intricacies. There were three metal loops attached to it.

Oh, fuck.

Just as the realization hit me, Saint appeared in the doorway, a chain wrapped around his wrists. Fuck.

Poe entered the bathroom last. He took the chain from Saint and nodded to Grim.

Grim exhaled, shuddering in anticipation as he opened my robe and slid it off my shoulders. He dragged the collar across my chest, using it to caress me, tracing circles around my swollen nipples with it. "I'm really going to enjoy seeing you like this," he rasped.

I stiffened. I'd be giving up more control. But wasn't that what I'd already done? From the moment I said yes, I gave them permission to own me. To do whatever the fuck they wanted to me. And that thought sent another burst of heat through my body.

I swallowed hard and lifted my chin, holding eye contact with Grim.

He chuckled as he wrapped the collar around my neck, fastening it at my nape. "Good girl."

It was tight but not choking me. Just tight enough to remind me who was in charge. Poe inched forward and tugged on my collar, causing me to stumble into him. He fingered the ring at the base of the collar, caressing it like it was a part of me. I guess now it was.

I drew in a sharp breath as he hooked one end of the chain into my collar. His eyes lit up with lust and desire. As he stepped back so all three of them could admire me, the other end wrapped tightly in his fist, I became dizzy. An animalistic need inside my belly bloomed. They were beasts, and I was at their mercy.

Saint took the chain from Poe and tugged me forward to his chest. "Beautiful," he growled. "Ours."

He pulled me out of the bathroom and away from the living room, down the hall. Grim and Poe followed close behind. I could feel their warm breaths on my back. Fuck, I was so wet.

They herded me to my bedroom. The blankets and pillows had been stripped off my queen size bed. Only the top sheet remained. I shivered.

Saint stood behind me. He tugged on my chain and backed me up into his hard cock. I couldn't help my body for wanting to feel him. I wiggled against his crotch, and his hand shot forward as he cupped my pussy.

"Please," I begged.

"Get on the bed," he ordered in his low gruff voice.

I nodded as he gave me some slack on the chain to climb onto the bed. As soon as my knees hit the mattress, he tugged back on the chain again. "No. I want your head at the foot of the bed."

I laid back against the squishy mattress and inhaled a deep breath.

Poe came to one side of the bed and removed his shirt, then his pants. He was gorgeous with abs that rivaled Grim's. How were all three of them so fucking perfect?

Grim came to the other side. The three of them gazed down at me, their lips wet and cocks hard. "Let's play, little fox."

He climbed onto the bed and ran a hand up the length of my thigh. Moisture pooled out of my folds. I bit back a whimper as he stroked my wet slit. Saint handed him the chain right before he grabbed my wrists and held them tight above my head. Oh, fuck. Poe growled in need as he joined us on the bed.

Grim stuck his finger deep inside his mouth and pulled it out slow. Without warning he shoved it into my tight pussy. I clenched and bucked my hips. "Relax, beautiful." He held his finger still inside me. My clit throbbed.

Poe massaged my belly. "*Let's see how wide you can stretch for us.*"

Grim fisted his cock, rubbing the tip of it against my

aching folds. "Beg for it. Tell me how bad you fucking want it."

I wanted to touch it. I tried to pull away from Saint, but he held my wrists tighter.

Poe pushed on my nub while Grim teased me with his tip, stroking it up and down my dripping wet entrance. "Fucking say it, or I'll just torture you like this all night."

I panted, the need to feel him inside me taking over every other thought. "Please... I need it. I fucking need it so bad. Please, Grim."

A sinister smirk played across his lips. "Good girl." He teased at my entrance, pushing himself halfway in. "Relax... open up for me."

I spread my legs wider, and he inched in farther, gasping as I clenched around him. Shit he felt so fucking good.

Poe moaned and sucked on my nipples while Saint panted behind me, holding my wrists firm.

Grim slid in and out of me slowly as he moved deeper into me. He was so big I could feel him in my fucking back. I rocked my hips into him, letting him hit every angle.

I cried out as he hit my spot, sparkly spots clouding my vision. "Oh, fuck...Grim."

"Fuck yeah, scream my name, you dirty girl. Such a good fucking dirty little fox." He pounded into me harder, faster. He rose up, towering over me as he thrusted, pulling on my leash. He came inside me as I unraveled underneath him.

Grim pulled out and laid back next to me. "So fucking good."

I could barely catch my breath before Poe was on top of me, sucking on my pebbled nipples. "I want in, little fox."

Staring up at his cold blue eyes, a little tremor shot through me. I was ready for more. I was insatiable. They had awoken something in me that would not be dormant any longer.

I licked my lips and spread my legs wide again, arching my hips toward him in offering.

Poe growled at the gesture. "You are taking us so well. Fuck. I'm going to make you cum again. So hard."

He pushed at my slick entrance and we both gasped as his hard cock slid inside. I let out a moan as he drew back and then plunged forward through my clenched walls. I felt like I was flying. Saint still held my wrists tight in his hands, caressing them with his thick fingers. Next to me, Grim looked on, his cock hard again at the sight of me being fucked by Poe.

Grim grabbed my chain and tugged, pulling my face to his. He kissed me hard, shoving his tongue between my lips and exploring my eager mouth.

"Fuck, you make me so needy, little fox."

Poe moved deeper inside me, and I bucked. "Oh, fuck. Yes. Just like that," I cried out.

"Say my fucking name." He pounded harder.

I broke away from Grim's kiss. "Poe," I rasped. "You feel so fucking good."

"Uhh, fuck yeah." The whole bed shook as he pumped into me. While Grim was more sensual and slower with his movements, Poe was like an animal. He was unleashed. Wild. Raw. And I fucking loved it.

My pussy trembled as my orgasm built. The tingling spread through my thighs first, then my swollen clit, until finally it took hold of my entire body. I screamed out as it washed over me, clenching, and squeezing around him like I was trying to milk every last drop.

This triggered him, and he poured into me, digging his fingers deep into my hips to hold me still as he came.

My legs felt like dead weights. My pussy was raw. But I was feeling the highest I've ever felt.

Saint released my wrists just as Grim and Poe nuzzled up against me, each throwing a leg over one of mine.

I waited, my heart hammering, for Saint to move on me next. But to my surprise he left the room.

A wave of disappointment came over me. I was exhausted, sore, and emotionally spent, but the thought of him not wanting me had me reeling. Did he get his fill just by watching me? Did I do something that turned him off?

Moments later, I heard the rush of water coming from the bathroom. Grim chuckled. "Saint's ready for you, little fox."

Poe stroked the outside of my pussy, making me wet again. "Are you going to be a good girl and do exactly what he says?"

My breath hitched. So he did want me. I nodded. "Yes."

"That's what we like to hear," Grim breathed.

Saint stalked back into the room, grabbed my chain, and tugged me out of bed. I grasped onto it so as not to get choked. Although, I wasn't entirely opposed to that either. What was wrong with me?

Saint led me into the hot steamy bathroom and closed

the door behind us. I was confused. "They aren't joining us?" I was under the impression that they were a package deal.

He shook his head. "Not this part… get in the shower."

His eyes were dark, sinister. I swallowed hard, suddenly afraid of what he was going to do. As I turned around and stepped into the tub, he shoved me against the wall. My breasts pushed up against the cold tile, hardening my nipples. I was starting to think they'd be permanently swollen at this point.

"Don't move," he ordered in his gruff voice.

I don't know what I was expecting, but it wasn't this. I felt the fuzzy sponge at my back as he dragged it across my skin. The soapy suds oozed down my body. He was cleaning me.

"Turn around."

I gulped and slowly inched around to face him. He stood in front of me, fully naked. His body was covered in tattoos. Beautiful patterns of black and gray ink. And his cock, holy shit. I thought Grim and Poe were big. Saint was colossal. And the tip of it was pierced with a silver bar bell. I could only imagine what that would feel like inside me.

"Spread your legs."

I widened my stance and leaned back against the shower wall.

He pressed the sponge to my pussy, moving it up and down my slit. Broad strokes that turned to small circles as the soft foamy sponge tickled every nerve ending. I bit back the urge to moan. Saint seemed to like the quiet. He never broke eye contact with me as he worked the sponge over me like it was his own hand.

Despite just getting fucked by two of the hottest men I'd ever seen, this act that Saint was doing was more erotic than anything else. It was seductive and carnal. He was cleaning me but somehow I felt dirtier.

We stared at each other without speaking. I bit down on my lip as another orgasm threatened to strangle me. I didn't want to even breathe wrong for fear that he'd stop.

Sensations of ecstasy came before I could stop them. My knees began to shake. A deep rumbling in my belly burst through. I could see the very faint beginning of a smirk catch on Saint's lips. The heat from his body only made it worse as he stepped closer toward me, pressing the sponge harder against my clit.

His lips grazed my ear as he whispered, "*Cum for me.*"

It was all the coaxing I needed. Without another thought, I arched back against the tiles and let my body have its release. He snaked his muscular arm around my waist to hold me up as every tingling sensation possible, took hold of me. I grabbed his wrist and thrusted into the sponge. "Fuck… Saint…oh my, fucking…I need you to touch me. I need your cock. Please… Saint."

He took my earlobe between his teeth and gently bit down. Dropping the sponge, he cupped my pussy with his wet soapy hand. He drew in a sharp breath as I continued to grind against him. I ached for him so bad.

I was starving for him. Without thinking, I reached for his cock. He growled and wrapped a hand around my throat, threading his fingers through my collar. His grip tightened. "On your knees, fox."

Oh, fuck. He was so hot.

I got on my knees without hesitating. He yanked on my chain and shoved his cock into my mouth. I moaned into him as he squeezed my chin. His other hand moved to the back of my head. He grabbed a fistful of my hair and guided my mouth back and forth. Tears welled in my eyes as I struggled to breathe.

"Good girl," he rasped. He fingered my lips as I stretched my mouth wide around his throbbing cock. He tasted like ecstasy. I twirled my tongue around the barbell, and he shuddered, digging his fingers deeper into my scalp. He pulled at my hair until I flinched from the pain. But it hurt so fucking good.

He thrusted into me faster. I looked up and our eyes locked. The devil lived in his gaze. Cold, sinister, hard... *hungry*. My vision blurred as he hit the back of my throat. I choked back a sob as he fucked my mouth hard. I couldn't breathe, but he tasted so fucking good. I kept my eyes on his. I wanted him to see me take it.

His body jerked as he reached his peak. I saw it happen. The change in his eyes. The rush of blood to the tip of his cock which caused him to clutch the back of my head so tight I couldn't move. He held me still as his cum rushed into my mouth like a dam bursting. He moaned, deep and guttural. I cupped his swollen balls as he rode his orgasm, pumping it into my mouth. I swallowed every fucking drop.

He pulled me from my knees and lifted me up in his arms. I wrapped my legs around his waist as he pushed me up against the wall. "It's been so long..." He tapped his fist three times against the wall.

I heard the door open. Grim and Poe pulled back the

shower curtain and their eyes lit up. "Can we watch now?" Grim asked.

Saint grunted and gave them a nod. He lifted me out of the shower and carried me back into the bedroom. He set me down and then crawled onto the bed. "Get on top of me."

I was horny again for this man. What the actual fuck? I didn't even think it was possible to have this many orgasms.

As I climbed onto the bed, I felt Grim, and Poe come in behind me. I crawled on top of Saint, straddling him.

Grim joined us on the bed, his chest pressed against my back. I drew in a sharp breath as he reached around and fisted Saint's cock. He squeezed it in his palm and stroked up and down. Saint growled, "Put it in."

Oh, fuck. Grim pushed at my entrance with the tip of Saint's cock and I almost came right there. He guided it inside me, as I stretched for him. "Oh, shit. So fucking big," I murmured.

Grim lifted my hips up and down on Saint's cock. It was unbelievable. Indescribable. To feel another man behind you, moving your body, making you ride another man's cock. I almost blacked out. The three of us moved in a rhythm. Poe moved around to watch, fisting his own cock up and down as he looked on.

Grim's hands were everywhere—squeezing my nipples, pressing on my clit, sliding underneath, between us. He hoisted me up so he could wrap one of his hands around Saint's shaft while leaving the tip still inside me. He stroked him as he brought me down on him. Saint moaned. "Fuck... Grim and our little fox," he breathed.

Grim pulled me back against him as I rode Saint harder. I couldn't get enough. It would never be enough.

I had fucked all three of them. As another orgasm claimed me, panic rushed through my chest. They said they couldn't move on until they had all had sex with me. And now they had. But I didn't want them to leave. I didn't want to be alone. Without them… how would I ever feel pleasure like this again?

Saint unhooked the chain and removed my collar right before the four of us passed out on each other, a pile of tangled limbs and heaving chests.

CHAPTER Seven

For the first time since they'd arrived, there was a silence between us. A quiet understanding that we belonged to each other. And a deep sense of dread that we'd soon be ripped apart.

In all of my life I had never experienced anything like this. Something so depraved and vile and yet utterly beautiful at the same time. I had dreamed of it. But after being told my fantasies were dirty, I'd locked all those thoughts away.

But Grim, Poe, and Saint… they accepted me. Their desires matched mine. It wasn't wrong to want them. I *couldn't* believe it was wrong to want them. To want this. Forever.

I put clothes on, actual clothes, for the first time since they'd arrived. I sat down at my kitchen table in a T-shirt, shorts, and fuzzy slippers. With their clothes back on as well, they seemed to tiptoe around me.

Saint set a steaming cup of coffee in front of me. Without complaining I shuffled to the cabinets and grabbed sugar. He tracked my movements, observing everything I did even as I went to the fridge to retrieve the milk.

I didn't want to offend him, but after the night I had, I was going to take my coffee the way I wanted it. Just like they took what they wanted.

Grim sat at the windowsill, the same one he'd first violated me on. He stared out the window as the October mist came down on my driveway. I wondered what he was thinking. How long would they stay?

Maybe I could cook them breakfast or dinner or something. Fuck. Did they even eat food? What in the hell was I thinking? That I could do normal things with three demonic spirits that invaded my home?

Yes, they gave me the best fucking erotic night of my life, but they aren't my boyfriends. This wasn't an episode of The Vampire Diaries. Hell, I don't recall Elena ever getting railed by three guys in the same night. So yeah, reality was setting in fast.

But I wasn't ashamed. No. I enjoyed it. I fucking loved it. And when they left, I would remember it forever. I'd never fully enjoy regular sex ever again, but that was okay because for one vicious night, I got to live out my wildest fantasies. And that would have to be enough.

"We don't want this to end, little fox," Poe blurted out, cutting the silence like a knife.

I drew out a long-held breath. "I don't want you to go."

There, I said it out loud. I couldn't bear the thought of not having them here with me.

Grim's shoulders' heaved. "We *have* to go… *but* no one can stop you from coming with us. If you want…"

Saint growled. "*No*. She has her life to live."

"Wait, you're suggesting that I go back to Wickford with you? It's condemned. The city is tearing it down next week." I hadn't even thought about what would happen to them when that happens.

Saint gave Poe a look as he protested. "You're such a good girl, little fox."

"The best girl," Grim added.

Poe leveled his gaze on me. "Once the house is destroyed, there will be no reason for us to stay. This is it, little fox. Our one last hurrah. I'm happy it was you…"

Fuck. This was crazy. I've spent less than twenty-four hours with them, and I was already growing attached. I let these monsters in my bed. In my house. In my life. I made that decision when I broke into Wickford. Despite my skepticism, a small part of me knew the superstition could be real.

Ever since I was a kid, strange things happened around me. I always had a sixth sense. Crows and black clouds seem to follow me everywhere I went. While my family has long since passed away from this life, my connection to them has remained. They come to me in dreams. A part of me wanted to awaken something last night.

I was tired of being alone…

"What if I was able to stop the city from tearing the house down, could you stay?" I finally understood everything that has led up to this moment.

"And how would you do that, Bailey?" Saint growled.

"I could buy it," I replied.

The three of them exchanged a worried look. Grim rested a hand on my waist. The warmth from his fingers tingled my skin. "Can you?"

My heart was racing. I nodded. "When my parents died, they left me a pretty good chunk of money. I haven't touched any of it. Was saving it for some reason. Now I know why. I could buy the house and have it restored. We could live there… together."

Poe ran a hand through his dark hair. "You would do that for us? Why? We came in here and defiled you."

I choked back a sob. They had no idea. "No. You liberated me. Set me free. Now that I've tasted it, I want more. I don't want it to ever stop."

Saint laced his fingers through mine. "You're young, little fox. Your tastes will change. And when they do, you'll wish you hadn't kept us."

I shook my head. "No. I will always be happy I kept you… But maybe, you'll grow tired of me. Is that what's holding you back? Will you grow bored of me?"

The three of them rushed forward at the same time, each placing a strong hand on me. Grim cupped my chin in his hands. "Never. In the hundred years we've been imprisoned, not a single person has seen us the way you have. You have given us so much more than flesh, little fox. Your warmth and care are more than we've ever known."

My chest ached. "You said you were poisoned. What happened? I think I've earned the right to know."

Poe motioned for me to take a seat on the couch. "We were tricked," he murmured.

I tucked my legs underneath me, pulling my robe down around my knees. Goosebumps pebbled my flesh. "Who did that to you?"

Grim sat on the coffee table across from me. "We worked for Mrs. Wickford. She was a widow who lived there all by herself. I maintained the house while Saint oversaw the grounds and Poe cooked all her meals. She gave us room and board, and a small weekly salary."

Saint sighed as he sank into the seat next to me. "She was a reclusive woman. No one ever visited, and she never left. She spent most of her time in the garden, humming to herself."

"But after a while," Poe interjected, "she took more of an interest in us, inviting us to eat dinner with her and joining her by the fire at night for drink and conversation. She was a lonely woman."

"And she was very beautiful," Grim added.

A slight twinge of jealousy panged me as I imagined my guys doting on this woman. It was silly, but my heart had started the process of claiming them. And I couldn't stop it.

"It wasn't long after that she started visiting us at night in our rooms as we slept," Poe continued. "Her carnal appetite was insatiable. She grew very attached to all of us. And we attached to her. But something snapped in her one day…"

A shiver crept up my spine. "What happened?"

Saint's face paled. "She lost her fucking mind."

Grim squeezed his hand. "An old woman started coming around. A witch. She fed into her delusions. Told her that we could live forever."

I gasped. "*No*… Fuck."

Poe nodded. "Fuck is right. She refused to get help. To see a real doctor. So we told her we were leaving. That we wanted no part in her witchcraft."

I leaned forward, riveted. "How did she react?"

Saint snickered. "Mrs. Wickford gave us her blessing and invited us to one last dinner."

A cold chill swept through me. So cold I could feel it in my bones. "*Poison*," I whispered.

Grim drew in a sharp breath. "All four of us died that night. On Samhain—Halloween. But only the three of us were stuck inside that house for eternity."

"She left us a note," Poe started. "That if she couldn't have us, no one could. At least not forever. The veil between the living and the dead would drop for one night only. If someone with intent was able to open the door to that cursed room, then we could leave. But her witch fucking cursed us."

Saint nodded. "There was a catch. We would be tied to the person who opened the door. And in order for our spirits to release them, to return to the house, we'd have to get their permission to defile them. Otherwise, we'd be trapped in nothingness."

"The Wickford house is our home," Grim added, "and it's the devil we know."

Tears streamed down my cheeks before I could stop them. "You're safe now. I will save your house and keep you for as long as you want to be kept."

CHAPTER Eight

"We belong to you now, little fox. There's only a few more hours left and then we must go." Grim untied my robe and pushed it open, putting me on display.

My breath hitched. "And I will join you as soon as I get everything in order."

Poe licked his lips as he pressed his palms into my thighs. "Let us have one more taste to keep us going."

Fuck, I wanted them again. And again. So fucking bad. I spread my legs and arched my back against the couch. "I'm yours to do whatever you want with now."

Saint growled and lifted me into his lap. His cock stiffened underneath me. He unzipped his pants and pulled it out. I gasped as he grinded against my bare ass. "So fucking responsive for us."

A smirk pulled at Grim's lips. "Let's play one more game then, little fox. A preview of what's to come."

I let out a groan as Poe slid a thick finger inside my sopping wet pussy. "Oh, fuck. Yes, I want to play. *Please*."

"Good girl," Saint breathed in my ear.

Grim grabbed my wrists and yanked me up. "Get on the floor. On your hands and knees."

Moisture pooled between my legs. My nipples pebbled. What wicked things did they have in store for me now? I lowered myself to the floor and did as he said.

They circled me.

"Spread your legs nice and wide for us, little fox," Poe commanded.

Fuck, I was going to cum before anything even started. I lowered myself farther down, bracing against the hardwood floors with nothing but my bare hands and knees.

"So fucking filthy for us, aren't you?" Grim asked, his voice low and raspy.

My breath quickened. "Yes."

"Let's show her what happens to dirty girls." Grim slid the collar back around my neck and gave the chain a good tug.

I was practically salivating. My juices dripped down my thighs. The anticipation, not knowing what was about to happen, was just as arousing as what they had already done to me.

Poe kneeled down next to me and grabbed my chin, forcing me to look into his piercing green eyes. "Give me a word, little fox. Something you'll remember."

I blinked a few times, mesmerized by his long black lashes. "Why?"

Grim knelt down on the other side of me and yanked my chin away from Poe. Now I was drowning in pools of blue eyes, colder, harder, but just as fucking hungry. "Because the lines between pleasure and pain are about to blur for you. We need to know when you've had enough."

Oh fuck. I should have been terrified. But all it did was make me wetter. Needier. "Okay, my word is... *devil.*"

Grim's smirk deepened. "Good girl." He looked at Poe. "You're up first."

Saint pulled up a chair and sat in front of me, holding tight to my chain. "I want to hear you scream, little fox."

I swallowed hard, my heart racing. Fuck, fuck, fuck. What am I doing?

I turned my head to the side just in time to see Poe pick up the leather riding crop. He slid it back and forth against his palm. He stalked around me dragging the tip of the crop down my spine as he circled until finally stopping behind me. I clenched my pussy as he tickled my ass with it, caressing me gently.

He chuckled as I flinched every time it touched me. He teased me for what seemed like hours, stroking it down the middle of my ass. My legs trembled in anticipation.

And just when I thought I was going to collapse onto the floor, the wind changed above me. I heard the snap before I felt the sting.

"Fuckkk," I cried out.

He smacked the other side of my ass, harder this time,

and I bucked forward. The sting spread, shooting tingles throughout my entire body.

Grim rubbed my back. "Good girl."

My eyes watered as Poe brought the crop down harder. Then the warm flesh of his palm was on me. He kneaded my ass gently. "You like it, don't you?"

I gasped for breath. I fucking loved it. "Yes," I whispered.

Saint pulled my chain. "Louder."

"Yessss," I cried out.

"My turn," Grim growled. He sat down on the edge of the windowsill. "Come here, little fox."

My body was shaking. I started to push myself up when Poe cracked the whip down hard again. "No. Dirty girls don't get to stand up. Fucking crawl to him."

Oh, fuck. I was almost ashamed of how turned on I was. *Almost*. But they didn't make me feel any shame. No. They make me feel alive.

Saint unhooked my collar and patted me on the head. "Such a good fucking girl. Go to him. Nice and slow."

I locked eyes with Grim. His gaze was darker, hungrier than before. I watched him watching me as I crawled across the floor to him. He took off his jeans but held onto his belt. My pussy was aching with need by the time I reached him.

Grim laid back against the window. "Lay across my lap."

I crawled up and onto him, trembling. As soon as I stretched out across him, he grabbed my wrists and fastened them tight behind me with his belt. His hard cock pulsed against my stomach. "Relax, little fox. I'm going to make you cum so fucking hard and for so fucking long, you might not ever be able to stand up straight again."

I shuddered as he dragged the tip of his fingers down the opening of my ass. "I like to feel the sting against my hand," he rasped.

He trailed his fingers further down, cupping my pussy in the palm of his hand. "Fuck, you are wet. So fucking filthy."

I moaned as he squeezed my clit. "Grim...*please*."

His cock throbbed against my abdomen. He pushed a finger inside me but held it still. "Say it again, little fox. Beg me."

I writhed against him. "Please make me cum, Grim."

Without warning he brought his palm down hard against my ass. "Again."

A deep guttural moan escaped my lips as he pushed another finger inside me. I clenched around him, squirming to try and get myself off against him.

"Please, fuck. I want to cum. Grim, please."

He growled and hit my ass again. I screamed as it reverberated through my entire body. He shoved his fingers deeper inside. Stars clouded my vision. Sweat pooled down my back. "Ughhh, fuck... yes." I panted.

I turned my head to see Poe and Saint fisting their own cocks, and I cried out again. I had almost completely forgotten that we weren't the only two in the room. The sight of them touching themselves pushed me over the edge.

The pressure swelled against the walls of my pussy. "Grim. Fuck. I'm... I'm close."

Grim slowed the rhythm of his fingers to an agonizing

pace, drawing it out like torture. My senses were heightened. My nerves tender and raw. I could feel every inch of his fingers from the soft tips as they reentered, all the way past the second knuckle as he stretched me. The slickness as they slid back and forth. I rocked my hips against him and spread my legs, allowing him to go even deeper. It was pure fucking ecstasy.

"That's it. Just like that, little fox." He fisted my hair and turned my head back toward Poe and Saint. "Show them what a good girl you are and cum for us…"

And that's what sent me over.

I clenched and gasped as my orgasm took hold of my nub first and then spread deep inside. As I moaned through the pleasure, Grim brought his hand down hard on my ass. I flinched and another orgasm rippled through me.

"Fuck," I screamed.

Grim stroked my back as I shook. He untied my wrists as he leaned down and whispered in my ear, "I want you to feel your cum dripping all over my cock. It feels so fucking good. So dirty."

I struggled for breath as my heart pounded out of my chest. I reached in between us and wrapped my hands around his cock. He moaned as I stroked him, smearing my sticky juices up and down his shaft.

Poe growled and stalked over to us. "Turn her over."

As I was flipped around, I kept my hand firmly on Grim's cock. Poe stood over me as he touched himself. "Open your mouth."

I parted my lips just as he shoved his cock inside. "Good fucking girl." He grabbed the back of my head as he fucked my mouth. I kept my grip on Grim, sliding my hand up and down to the rhythm of Poe. "Fuck." A burst of liquid hit the back of my throat as he moaned. I drank every drop of his thick warm cum. And then another burst coated my fingers as Grim released. He bucked against the window, nearly breaking it.

I licked my lips and smiled up at Poe. "You taste so fucking good."

Every inch of my flesh was on fire.

"I want her back on the floor," Saint commanded. He stood from the couch and stepped out of his jeans.

Fuck. I almost forgot there were three of them. I was on the verge of blacking out. The stimulation was driving me crazy. But no matter how battered I was, I would not resist Saint. I needed him to touch me. I wanted him to make me cum so bad.

Poe and Grim lifted me up and placed me gently on the floor on my back. Saint picked up the riding crop and stalked over to me.

I was getting spanked again. I clenched my pussy as a new wave of tingling started to spread. I started to climb back onto my hands and knees when Saint grabbed my ankles.

"No. I don't want you on your knees, little fox. Not this time."

I was confused. "What are you going to do?"

His eyes glazed with carnal desire as he stared at my pussy. "Remember your word?"

Poe and Grim moved behind me and each grabbed one of my wrists.

"Y-yes. I think so."

Saint dragged the riding crop over my hard nipples. "Say it so I know you didn't forget."

I inhaled a sharp breath. The feel of the leather crop against my swollen nipples was amazing. "*Devil*," I rasped.

"Good girl. Now open up nice and wide for me."

I spread my thighs as far as they would go, feeling the beginning of an orgasm starting to already move through me. Sometimes, the fantasy, the waiting, could make me cum without even a single touch.

Saint circled the riding crop around my nipples one last time and then slowly trailed it down my stomach. I watched him as his gaze devoured every inch of my body. He shifted the crop farther down, teasing it over my swollen nub. I let out a little whimper.

"Look at that glistening cunt. So wet and ready for all the dirty things I'm about to do to it."

I shivered as he dragged the edge of the crop between my wet folds. He gently nudged it against the lips of my pussy, using it as a tool to peel back my flesh. I was coming undone underneath it. The leather felt so fucking good. So smooth against me.

I couldn't help myself from arching up to meet it, urging him to rub harder. I needed more pressure. "Don't stop," I pleaded.

"Do you like my toy, little fox?" Saint rasped.

My teeth chattered. "Y-yes. Play with me, please."

Grim growled as he took one of my nipples between his fingers and squeezed. Poe followed suit and grabbed the other one. Fuck. I was going to black out if I didn't cum soon.

Saint lifted the crop away and brought it back down with a light slap.

Oh, fuck. I bucked as the slap sent a shiver deep down inside my pussy. I couldn't stop my body from trembling. But I needed more. "Again," I begged.

Saint slowly rubbed the crop against my clit, applying more pressure this time. I rocked against it, aching to feel that sting again. Before I could beg some more, he lifted up and brought it down again, smacking the inside of my dripping wet pussy.

This one fucking stung. But it also felt like heaven. A tiny orgasm shot through me as I clenched. I writhed on the ground while Poe and Grim held me firmly in place. I squeezed my eyes shut for a moment and saw stars.

The stinging began to fade, and it turned me ravenous. "*Harder*," I breathed.

Saint let out a low growl. He pressed the leather crop to my clit again, rubbing me back and forth till I was almost raw. "Such a good girl."

I screamed as the leather riding crop came down hard against my wet pussy. An orgasm unlike any I've ever known took hold of me, pulling me down like quicksand. Sparks of light burst through my closed lids as I tore out of Poe and Grim's grasp. Like a wild animal, I pounced on Saint.

"That's it, little fox. Take what belongs to you." Saint stretched back onto the floor as I straddled him and rode out my orgasm on him.

He dug his thick fingers into my hips as I clenched

around him. "Fuck me hard, little fox. Give me everything you've got."

And I did. I bounced up and down his slick cock, twisting and grinding till I could feel him in my stomach.

The second my cum coated his shaft, he lost it. He squeezed my ass, lifted me into the air, and took me against the wall. "Dirty. Fucking. Girl. *Fuck.*"

He held me still against him as his cum dripped down my thighs.

Poe and Grim were at our side within minutes. With Saint's cock still pulsing inside me, Grim grabbed my chin and placed a hungry kiss on my lips. He shoved his tongue deep into my mouth while Saint moaned against me. He slid in and out as he came. Poe reached his hand in between us and stroked my clit.

Grim broke the kiss to look down at our bodies sliding together. He watched as Saint's cock moved in and out. Watched Poe finger my nub, as another orgasm began to build inside me.

Grim stuck his finger in my mouth. "Get it nice and wet for me."

I moaned as I sucked on his finger, coating it with as much saliva as I could muster.

He pushed at the entrance to my ass, and I clenched. He drew in a sharp breath. "Relax, little fox. Let me in."

I gasped as he inched his finger farther in. "Oh, fuck."

"That's it. Just like that," he coaxed as I started to relax and give in.

Saint screamed as he came. A burst of cum shot through me. I thrusted into Saint, arching my hips up.

Poe pinched my clit. "Surrender to it, little fox.

"Yes," I cried out.

And as another orgasm rippled through me, Grim pushed his finger all the way in.

If I had neighbors, they would have called the cops. That is how fucking loud I screamed. And it was the most satisfying scream of my entire life.

The four of us leaned into each other, our chests heaving, bodies glistening with sweat. We held each other up. Gave each other breath.

I hugged them tight to me.

I knew one thing for sure… I was never letting them go.

CHAPTER *Nine*

There was only an hour left till dawn. Halloween would be over, and they would have to return to Wickford. And I would have to act fast to buy it before the city tears it down. My friends would think I'm crazy, but I didn't care. They would never understand. While they were preoccupied with jello shots and toilet papering houses, I was here with Saint, Grim, and Poe, being reborn. Having the best night of my life.

They stood near my front door, waiting to say goodbye. I looked the three of them over with a fresh gaze. When they first arrived, I'd thought them monsters. Now they were my saviors. They had dragged me kicking and screaming from my old life and awakened the darkest pleasures within me.

Dusk was almost fading away. The sun would rise soon and so they had to go. Poe clasped the back of my neck and pressed his forehead to mine. "Little fox... Fuck. What a surprise you were."

I brushed my lips to his. He kissed me with a fire that sent shivers up my spine. His soft tongue gently twirled around mine. I clung to him in desperation, fisting my hands in his hair. "I will see you soon," I murmured.

Grim pulled me out of Poe's arms and into his. He gazed down at me with those piercing blue eyes that I was once afraid of. Eyes that rooted me in place and commanded my body to do things not even my wildest fantasies could dream up.

He stroked my hair. "In case... something goes wrong... just know that I'll never forget you."

I shook my head. "Nothing will go wrong. I will see you soon. I promise."

He bent down and placed a soft kiss on my lips. "Whatever you say, little fox."

I almost crumbled at Saint's feet. His lips were pursed, his expression unreadable. But his eyes... were full of sadness and longing. I stood in front of him, unsure of how I was going to part from him. From any of them.

Saint yanked my hips to his. My nipples pebbled at the feel of his chiseled chest pressed up against mine. There would never come a day when I didn't want him. He kissed my neck, my jaw, then finally my lips.

"You're such a good girl, Bailey. The world has no idea.

Thank you for trusting us. Remember us. Remember this night. And know that you can do anything you want. Anything you set your mind to."

Tears streamed down my cheeks. "You weren't the only ones locked in a prison. While I may have been able to roam around, I was captive just the same. Thank you for setting me free."

They circled me and pulled me into a group hug. Our breaths were heavy. I couldn't discern whose heart was beating louder. We were like one symbiotic unit. I felt like I was losing a part of myself right now.

Some believe in love at first sight. Others believe that lust can be confused with love. I don't know what the clinical definition of love is. I just know that it's messy and imperfect and life changing. There are no rules on who one should love or how long it should take to fall. Love is intangible. It cannot be grasped with human hands or even understood with rational thought.

Would I call what we did love? I don't know. It was something like love. It was definitely lust and desire and passion. Isn't that how love starts? Looking at the three of them lingering in the doorway, still smelling their mingled scents on my skin, something did stir and ache in my heart. Call it longing or pheromones or even foolish fantasy, it doesn't matter what it is. It makes me feel alive. That's all that matters. And I will not let it go. I won't let them go.

"I will call my attorney. She can get the funds from my trust in order and make an offer on the house today. Once the deed is mine, I'll make plans to renovate. To make it a home again. And then we can all be together… for as long as you want me." I sniffled and wiped the remaining tears off my cheeks.

Poe flashed me a grin. "Ok, little fox. See you soon."

Grim nodded. "Till we meet again."

This felt like goodbye. No. I would make this work. It had to work. I couldn't lose them. Before new tears threatened to fall again, Saint pulled me in for one last hug.

"We will wait for you, Bailey. For as long as we can," he whispered.

I nodded, choking back a sob. Poe opened my front door, and as each one of them stepped through it, a piece of my heart went with them. Saint paused and looked back one more time. He winked and then closed the door behind him.

Out of the corner of my eye, I spotted the duffel bag they'd come in with. The bag of toys that we had so devilishly played with. I grabbed it and threw open the door.

"Wait, you forgot—" I sank to my knees. Fuck. They were gone. I scanned the yard, the trees that lined the path leading up to my house. There was no sign of them. If I hadn't had this bag in my hands, I might even start to think I'd hallucinated the whole thing.

I went back inside and sank down on the couch, the bag in my lap. I clung to it as the one last piece I had of them. My house was eerily quiet. I used to love that. Not anymore. It was just a cruel reminder that I was alone.

A buzzing noise came from my bedroom. Fuck, my phone. I hadn't touched it in over twenty-four hours. I darted into my bedroom and retrieved it from the bedside table.

Ten missed calls and twenty-five texts. All from Maureen. Shit. I scanned through the messages. Most of them were drunken commands to get my ass to the party. The last five were more of the—where are you bitch; I'm worried about you—variety.

I sighed and texted her back.

Hey Maureen, sorry I didn't respond. I took a sleeping pill and passed out. No need to worry. Hope you had fun at the party.

The typing bubbles appeared immediately.

Oh, thank god! After what happened at Wickford, and then not hearing from you, I thought you actually got kidnapped by ghosts! Meet for coffee later?

If only she knew.

I sent back a quick reply.

Haha. No such thing as ghosts, Maureen. Yeah, let's meet up this afternoon. I need to run a few errands in town anyway.

I was pretty sure the whole town, including my well-meaning friend, will think I'm nuts when they find out I'm buying a condemned and supposedly haunted house. I was dreading even having the conversation. But I know in my heart that this is what I want. It's the first time in my life that I've known exactly what I wanted.

Two weeks later

My attorney, Evelyn, pushed her glasses higher up her nose. "Okay, Miss Bishop, just sign here and the house is yours. It took a bit of convincing, but the city decided that it was in their best interest to make money off of the house rather than *spend* money tearing it down."

I nodded and picked up a pen, my hand trembling. This was it. Wickford was mine. *Poe, Grim, and Saint were mine.*

Evelyn scooped up the paperwork and stuck it in a file. "I'll finalize everything today and get the ball rolling for the reconstruction. It will not be easy, but by this time next year, you should be living in your new home."

The sound of that sent a warm ripple through my body. "Thank you, Evelyn. I appreciate all you've done for me since my parents died."

She smiled curtly. "Of course."

I couldn't get out of her office fast enough. I dashed to my car and headed directly to Wickford place.

I skidded into the driveway just as workers were removing the caution tape. A sold sign already sat in the front yard. I jumped out of the car and raced across the porch into the house. Pausing on the first floor, I looked around. It was just as cold and barren as it was two weeks ago. But I wasn't afraid anymore. It was already feeling like mine.

I barreled up the stairs to the second floor and down the hallway to the room my guys were locked in. The door was still broken from me losing my footing and crashing into it.

I crept inside. "Poe? Grim? Saint? Are you still here?"

The wind rustled one of the boards that were coming loose across the window. A crow squawked on the ledge. I hugged my arms to my chest as I stood in the dark room. Waiting.

My heart sank. It was so quiet. So empty. What if I had dreamed the whole thing up? Or what if they had finally passed over to the other side?

I choked back a sob and called out for them again. "I'm here. Like I promised."

The floorboards creaked behind me. Strong arms snaked around my waist. I breathed a sigh of relief as his scent enveloped me.

"Welcome home, little fox," Saint rasped.

I spun around and threw my arms around his neck. Behind him, Poe, and Grim stood smiling. "I thought maybe I had hallucinated all three of you." I held out my arms for them to come over. I hugged Poe and Grim tight to my chest. "I'm so happy to see you."

Poe brushed a strand of hair off my forehead. "We knew you'd come, little fox."

"Now we can always be together," Grim murmured.

I nodded. "The construction will take a while, but I don't care. I'm not leaving you again. I'll sleep on the broken floor with you."

Saint grinned. A rare expression from him. "Luckily, it won't come to that. There's a basement, Bailey. It was untouched by the fire. We have already prepared it for you."

Grim beamed. "It's our gift to you. You'll be comfortable there until the rest of the house is ready."

My heart wanted to burst. I was beyond happy for the first time in my life. Some people are lucky if they find love once in a lifetime. I have found it three times over.

I stepped back and admired them, taking my time to really study each and every inch.

The three of them exchanged a mischievous look and it sent a flutter to my belly.

"Are you ready to see what we have in store for you downstairs, little fox?" Poe asked.

"*Yes*." My arousal was growing by the second. "Fuck, yes, please," I breathed.

Saint curled his arm around my waist. "*Good girl*."

Epilogue

One year later

"Good morning, little fox." Poe nestled his face in my neck.

I yawned and stretched out my arms. "It's going to be a great morning."

Grim reached across Saint to squeeze my thigh. "Happy anniversary, love."

Saint pulled me onto his chest. "Come here, little fox. It's time for us to give you your gift."

Heat spread between my thighs. "But you've already given me so much," I rasped.

Wickford place was restored to its original glory ahead of schedule. For the last six months, the three of us have been enjoying the fruits of our labor. We do everything together.

From dancing in the kitchen to having dinner in the garden and defiling each other in every single room. Now, as we lay here in our king-size bed amidst the black satin sheets, tangled up in each other's arms, in *our* bedroom, I can't help but think back to the night we first met.

"Seems like we've known each other longer, doesn't it?" I asked as Grim's hand traveled farther up my thigh.

Poe nuzzled my nipple. "That's because we are connected body and soul. Now, stop talking," he teased. "There are better uses for that mouth of yours."

I let out a moan as Grim slipped a finger inside my wet pussy.

Saint twisted me onto my side and pulled me toward him. His hard cock pressed into my ass. "I'm going to fuck you so hard, little fox." He kissed the back of my neck, sending a shiver down my spine. "And then… I'm going to give you a good hard spanking for playing so hard to get that night."

Oh, fuck. I was so wet. "You're going to punish me for a year ago?" I asked coyly.

"Mmm… yes, little fox," Saint whispered. "No dirty deed will go unpunished."

Poe and Grim each grabbed one of my wrists as Saint flipped me over onto my stomach. "Spread your legs nice and wide for me, little fox."

I whimpered and did as he said. My clit ached as I waited for all the dirty things they were about to do to me.

Saint mounted me from behind. His hard cock

pressed at the entrance to my sopping wet pussy. "Such a good girl."

I cried out as he yanked my hips up and thrusted in hard. "*Fuck.*"

Grim rubbed his fingers in circles around my tingling clit. I rocked back and forth, desperate to consume what they were both giving me.

Saint fisted his hand in my hair and pulled it tight. "So fucking slick for me." He pulled out slow and then thrusted back in with a force so hard I bucked forward.

"Fuuck," I screamed.

Poe let out a growl. "Such a dirty girl." He pressed a finger into my ass, and I lost it. "That's it, little fox. Move your hips just like that."

I ground against them, panting, and twisting as their hands explored every crevice of my body. Saint pummeled into me without restraint, stretching me like a rubber band. I braced my hands against the headboard and pushed back into him, urging him deeper.

Saint dug his fingers into my hips, "Fuck. I'm going to cum."

And just as Saint exploded inside me, Poe inched his finger deeper into my ass while Grim lowered his head to my middle. My vision blurred and sparked as I felt his warm soft tongue pushing against my nub. He sucked and flicked as the tingling intensified. I cried out as my orgasm gripped me, sending wave after wave of euphoria throughout my entire body.

"Happy anniversary, little fox," Saint breathed as he moved off me.

I collapsed onto him. Poe and Grim nestled in close, our arms and legs tangled up in each other. My chest heaved as I fought to regain my breath. "Happy Halloween."

Poe chuckled. "It's the first one in a hundred years we don't have to worry or wonder if someone's going to open that door and let us out."

I cradled his arm to my stomach. "You will never be locked up again."

Grim stroked my cheek. "We are happy it was you, Bailey."

"You made this place a home again," Saint added.

I didn't know a year ago that I would fall in love with three deviant spirits. Even the night they left; I was afraid to call it love. But I knew then as I know now that love is exactly what we share. It might not be what other people's definition is, but it is ours. And because of Poe, Grim, and Saint, I would never feel shame for loving like this ever again.

I will always be their good girl.

Acknowledgements

Good Girl is my first why choose dark romance novella. First of what will hopefully be many. This book rushed out of me like a hurricane. I enjoyed every minute of writing it. It's not for the faint of heart so if you made it to the end, welcome to my dark and twisted romance journey.

I want to thank every reader, reviewer, and blogger for reading Good Girl. Your support means the world to me.

Thank you to my amazing editor Kat, of Kat's Literary Services. You were such a joy to work with and I can't wait to put more books into your capable hands.

Thank you to Sarah Paige for the hottest cover I could have asked for. It's perfect.

Thank you to Champagne Book Design for formatting Good Girl. You always do amazing work.

Thank you to all of my friends and family. I love each and every one of you.

And thank you to booktok for inspiring me to choose a darker road.

ABOUT THE *Author*

M Violet is a dark romance author with a flair for the dramatic. She likes whiskey, rainy nights, and writing by the fire. When she's not creating scorching hot villains for you to fall in love with, you can find her eating chocolate and binge watching her favorite shows.

Facebook: Authormviolet
Instagram: Authormviolet
Tik Tok: Authormviolet

M VIOLET
DARK & SINFUL ROMANCE

Printed in Great Britain
by Amazon

86781192R10057